Together

Jane Simmons

ORCHARD

For Cassy, Glenn, Poppy,
Pan and Sheba.

Mousse

NUT

ORCHARD BOOKS
Carmelite House
50 Victoria Embankment
London EC4Y 0DZ

First published in 2006 by Orchard Books
First published in paperback in 2007

Text and illustrations © Jane Simmons 2006

The right of Jane Simmons to be identified as the author
and illustrator of this work has been asserted by her in accordance
with the Copyright, Designs and Patents Act, 1988.

A CIP catalogue record for this book is available from the British Library.

ISBN 978 1 84616 288 6

3 5 7 9 10 8 6 4 2

Printed in China

Orchard Books
An imprint of Hachette Children's Group
Part of The Watts Publishing Group Limited
An Hachette UK Company
www.hachette.co.uk

When Mousse met Nut, it was raining.

"Hello," said Mousse.

"Hello," said Nut.

They smiled at each other.
The rain stopped and sunshine
broke through the clouds.

"What a wonderful day!"
said Mousse.

"Wonderful!" said Nut.

Every day the sun shone and
every day Mousse sat with Nut . . .

or walked with Nut . . .

or played and giggled with Nut.

"You're my best friend!"
said Mousse.
"You're mine!" said Nut.

Everything
was wonderful.

But one day, Nut jumped on top of a wall.
"I can't jump that high," cried Mousse. "Come down!"
"No, I like it up here!" said Nut.

Later, Mousse paddled in the water.
"I can't swim," frowned Nut. "Come out!"

"No, I love it in here!" said Mousse.

Soon, they couldn't agree on anything.

"It's too hot
in the sun."

"It's too cold in
the shade."

"You're too fast."

"You're too slow."

Mousse's best bone was . . . . too **big!**

Nut's favourite biscuit was . . . tiny!

"Let's play in my house," tried Mousse.

"It's horrible, muddy and cold," moaned Nut. "I like it this way," said Mousse.

"Let's play at my house," said Nut.

But it was too small.

Dark clouds gathered outside.
"You're not my best
friend any more,"
said Mousse, unhappily.
"You're not mine
then," said Nut.

Everything
was horrible.

"Goodbye," said Mousse.

"Goodbye," said Nut.

It started to rain.

Mousse swam alone . . .

walked alone . . .

and chewed
her bone alone.

Nut sat in the rain alone.

They both went home alone . . .

and missed each other more than ever.

It was still raining when
Mousse went to find Nut.

"I want to be friends
again," said Mousse.
"Me too!" said Nut.

They smiled at each other.
The rain stopped and sunshine
broke through the clouds.

"What a wonderful day!"
said Mousse.

"Wonderful!" said Nut.

From then on, every day,
Mousse and Nut sat together . . .

and played and giggled together.

Even though they did
different things...

they did them together.

Whether it was sunshine or rain . . .

every day was wonderful . . .

. . . and so was every night.